The
DOSS TREE

The
DOSS TREE

George Henry

THE DOSS TREE

This is a work of fiction. All of the characters, names, incidents and dialogue in this novel are either the products of the author's imagination or are used fictitiously. Some of the places and organizations are real, with the exception of Corporate Europe which is fictitious.

iUniverse books may be ordered through booksellers or by contacting:

iUniverse
1663 Liberty Drive
Bloomington, IN 47403
www.iuniverse.com
1-800-Authors (1-800-288-4677)

Cover and Design by S.D.Henry

ISBN: 978-1-4917-7813-5 (sc)
ISBN: 978-1-4917-7814-2 (e)

Print information available on the last page.

iUniverse rev. date: 10/08/2015

Contents

Chapter 1   A big lorry... 1

Chapter 2   'The Doss Tree in Danger'............................. 6

Chapter 3   'Look after me'..12

Chapter 4   Let battle commence.....................................16

Chapter 5   Find the Queen... 22

Chapter 6   Three Tasks 27

Chapter 7   A strange fire 32

Chapter 8   A gathering of armies................................... 36

Chapter 9   A dream...39

Chapter 10 A victory... 48

Chapter 11 Summon the Reds 52

Chapter 12 The Doss storm 57

Chapter 13 A revelation...63

Chapter 14 Like magic...67

A big lorry

The Doss Tree was described in the Ordnance Survey of Ireland Revision Name Book in 1858 as 'a very ancient and conspicuous ash tree named Doss Tree.' It is in fact more than four hundred years old is still very much alive and is actually an oak tree!! It is number 3594 on the list of great trees on this island of Ireland.

The precise meaning of the name 'Doss' has been lost through the ages. Local people sometimes call it the 'Cabin Tree' but no one can say where this name comes from either. One local historian believes that Doss has something to do with the land and perhaps it simply means 'of the land' - very appropriate for such an ancient tree which stands at the end of the Cargin Road right on the edge of Lough Neagh. It might also be that there was a 'Doss house' in the area, where homeless people were able to take shelter or that those same people took shelter under the great boughs of the tree and that was why they called it the 'Cabin Tree', it was their 'live cabin home'.

It is still marked on the OS map of today beside Pollan Bay on the northern shore of Lough Neagh, the largest freshwater lake in the British Isles.

This is an ancient and very peaceful land where people work long hours at farming and fishing. The main farming type is dairying although sheep are also reared further away from the lough shore. One of the local farmers employs a very clever but bad tempered donkey to lead his cattle to and from the fields. Eel fishing takes place from Spring to Autumn beginning with the brown eels and ending with the silver eels. A good living can be made from this, along with catching the very popular Pollan fish which, coated in batter and deep fried, are a delicacy in the local fish and chip shop.

It was because of the eel fishing that Corporate Europe started to cast jealous and greedy eyes towards the Lough. It wasn't enough that most of the eels caught were already exported to Europe. Research had recently been completed which seem to indicate that there were many more eels to be got from the Lough.

But, let's not get ahead of the story.

Our family are what are called 'blow-ins', or, in other small towns and villages in Ireland, we would be called 'runners'. It means simply that we arrive, settle down for a while, before we move on to somewhere else. Our family has two boys and a girl – Shane the eldest at eleven, Nathan is eight and Megan is almost seven. This is their story.

My wife and I work away from home a lot, in busy jobs which involve a lot of travelling. We came to John Damians' house, as it is called locally, in the Spring-time and we didn't realise then what a strange incident our children would witness and become part of.

To this day I'm not sure what happened - really happened!

School was over for the summer and Aunt Sally was staying with us to look after the children until we got time off from work for holidays. They had already met lots of the children who lived nearby with the exception of one girl called Dolores, who lived near the Doss Tree. Dolores never said very much and she certainly didn't play with the other children. Shane tried his best to get to know her but she always managed to keep him at a distance.

One day the children were playing "chases" around the Doss tree when Megan tripped, hurt her ankle and ended up in tears. Dolores who had been watching them from her house came over to ask if Megan was all right. Shane and Nathan didn't know what to do, but Dolores, who was a little older than Shane, said she would have a look at it. After examining Megans' ankle Dolores said it wasn't broken but might be badly sprained.

'If your older brother and I can lift you fireman style to our house, my Mum will put a cold compress on it and maybe a bandage, which should help.'

Dolores held Shane's hands and Nathan helped Megan sit on their hands with her arms round their necks. They carried her like a wounded heroine into Dolores's kitchen where her Mum was baking.

'Well what have we here?', she asked.

Dolores explained what happened. After another examination Dolores's mum agreed with her that nothing seemed to be broken. She placed a soothing cold compress on the ankle and Megan soon started to feel better.

'You're lucky you won't need a trip to the hospital. Be sure to tell your aunt and she can keep an eye on it until your mum gets home. If it's still bad then perhaps you'll get a trip to casualty. OK. Now lets's get you and your brothers a cool drink.'

Megan nodded her thanks.

When everyone was sipping their drinks Dolores's mum busied herself with her baking, again remarking on the fact that Dolores was always bringing some wounded animal home, but this was the first time she ever brought a wounded person home!

The children laughed.

'Yes she brought home a rabbit once which had got caught in a snare and we saved its foot, a raven with a broken wing that was able to fly again and a poor wee hedgehog which had got itself tangled in a ball of barbed wire. We needed her dad with his wire cutters to help but we managed to free it eventually, it was OK. The rarest of all was a beautiful baby Barn Owl which she found abandoned in the garage. For some reason it couldn't fly. It trusted Dolores and we took it to the **World of Owls** at Mount Shalgus Lane near Randalstown. Over the last few years we've lost count of all the strays she has picked up, looked after, and then released back into the wild. Sadly some don't survive and so Dolores has her own place in the garden where she lays them to rest. Dolores is very special but she doesn't realise it yet. Do you know children that she is the seventh daughter of a seventh daughter? In Ireland they say that a seventh son of a seventh son has a very special gift for healing. Dolores I don't think can do that but we all feel that she has some other special gift.'

Dolores was looking a bit uncomfortable with her mum talking like this and Shane noticing this asked rather pointedly of his sister. 'Is your ankle any better Megan 'cause we'd better go home and tell Aunt Sally?'

Megan mumbled that it did feel a bit better.

'OK let's go, we'll help you. Thanks Mrs Downey for the drinks. Megan?'

'Thanks Mrs Downey for fixing me up.'

'You're very welcome. Now go easy on that ankle and by tomorrow hopefully it will be a lot better. Take care now. Bye bye.'

Dolores came by the next day to ask how Megan was doing. Aunt Sally brought her into the big kitchen where Megan was stretched out on a large sofa.

'Your Mum's magic did the trick. My ankle is a lot better today, thanks again Dolores.'

'You're very welcome. Where are your brothers?'

'They said they were going over to Murray's farm to see the new calves. I don't know when they'll be back.'

At that moment Shane and Nathan came rushing into the kitchen.

'See, I told you it was Dolores.'

Shane gave Nathan a playful thump on his shoulder.

'Hi there', he said rather awkwardly.

Dolores started to blush and Shane blurted out 'We saw a big lorry with European flags on the side of it heading towards the lough shore.'

Dolores stared at him as if he had two heads.

'What's wrong? What did I say?'

A look of anguish had crossed her face, 'I must go now.'

With that she turned and almost ran out of the kitchen.

'What a strange girl she is. I just can't make head nor tail of her' said Shane shaking his head.

'She's maybe not so strange' said Aunt Sally, 'I think I read somewhere in the papers that some big organisation calling itself Corporate Europe had submitted plans for developing this part of Lough Neagh and I believe they have got the final go ahead to start work.'

Shane thought that sounded very exciting for there would be more new machinery to look at compared to the rather dull farming equipment they usually saw.

As if reading his thoughts Aunt Sally said 'It might be very exciting for some people but the peace and quiet and probably the environment down here would be changed forever.'

Nathan and Megan both chipped in with, 'Yea we don't want them spoiling our magic play land.'

Shane on reflection thought that perhaps it mightn't be very good after all.

'Maybe it won't happen. Dad says the number of times governments give the go ahead for something and then six months later they change their minds. He says it's all politics.'

Shane looked at Nathan and Megan's blank faces and thought, 'well I don't know what politics are either, but it always sounds important when Mum and Dad talk about it.'

'I'll ask Dolores later. She seemed pretty upset by the news about the lorry. Didn't she?'

They all nodded.

'The Doss Tree in Danger'

Megan's ankle was a lot better and she was able to hobble about. Nathan was teasing her saying she was playing it up to get more attention. Before an argument could start Aunt Sally scolded him and Shane for not spending some time with their sister.

'The pair of you can use the rest of the day, until your parents come home, playing games with Megan.'

Behind Aunt Sally's back Megan stuck her tongue out at her brothers.

Curiosity was killing Shane so that when dinner was finished he couldn't wait to ask his Mum and Dad about developments in the Ballynamullan townland.

His Mum told the whole story.

A new landing harbour was to be created at the site of the old one, much bigger so that it could take larger fishing boats. A new processing plant for the fish and the eels was to be built on the flat ground beside the harbour right on the lough shore. This meant that the eels and the fish would be distributed from the plant as a finished product and be sent all over Europe. It would create new jobs and help sustain the future for the local fishing industry. The plans were approved by the new coalition government at Stormont and work was to begin after the Twelfth of July holiday.

'If this is all supposed to be good Mum, why is Dolores so upset?' asked Shane.

'I don't know. I suppose since her home is practically right on the shore maybe they will have to move. Or perhaps she feels they may end up living next door to a noisy, smelly fish factory. I must admit I don't think that would be very nice.'

'And', Shane's Dad added 'it would spoil a unique and very beautiful area. But you needn't worry, we'll probably not be here forever. Life changes, things change, nothing ever stays the same.'

That night the three children had talked about how much they loved the freedom and safety of playing along the road and all around the Doss Tree and the shore. There were always swans or geese to see, ducks, coots, grey herons, flocks of plovers and starlings, thousands of swallows and house martins chasing the flies.

Speaking of which – the flies!

Well Lough Neagh, as we have said, is famous for its eels, pollan fish and its size but it is also famous for its May flies. Zillions and zillions of them! Swarming in huge numbers, that from a distance look like low black swirling funnel shape clouds. They can get into your ears and make a buzzing sound. If you stand in the centre of one of these clouds you would think you were in the middle of a giant room with hundreds of people whispering in low voices. In the hottest days in May the flies congregate in the cool shadowed areas like the east or north facing gable walls on houses. White houses can look almost black when covered in the flies! The children had laughed at this because as they were told by the locals, 'if there were no flies, there would be no eels or birds.' The May flies don't bite like mosquitoes or midges, but, for the local people they are a benign nuisance.

They all agreed that even with the flies Doss was magical and they didn't want it any different. Shane said he would go and see Dolores the next day and find out more about 'the development.'

'I kinda like her. She's different alright, not like the other girls who I think are a bit silly.'

Nathan laughed but said nothing and Megan said she would come too as her ankle was a lot better.

Next morning, with Megan still limping, the three children set off to find their new friend. Shane knocked on the back door and Dolores's mum called 'Come on in!'

'Hello Mrs Downey we came down to see Dolores. She Looked upset when she left our house yesterday.'

'Aye. I'm afraid it was a bad day and things will get worse. Nothing for you to worry about. My Dolores is tough, she'll bounce back. She's over at the Doss Tree, probably looking at the Lough which is why you didn't see her when you came down the road.'

'Thanks Mrs Downey and thanks again for the other day.'

'Take care now and no more falling over young Megan.'

As the children climbed over the gate they could see Dolores' legs sticking out from the tree pointing towards the lough. As they came round the tree Shane and Nathan quietly said hello and Megan asked how she was.

'I'm OK. How's your ankle?'

'It's a lot better but why were you so upset yesterday?'

'I know, sorry. You probably all think I'm weird but honestly I was hoping that yesterday wasn't going to happen. Now it has the Doss Tree is in danger.'

The three children almost shouted together 'The Doss Tree is in danger? How?'

'It's a long story, but it's to do with building a factory here.'

'Yea our Mum and Dad told us a little bit about it last night. But sure, they're not going to build just here. There're lots of places all along the shore which would be better,' said Shane.

'Of course there are but the fact that there is already a small jetty for landing the eels here means that a precedent has been set.'

'What's a precedent?' asked Nathan.

'Well my Dad said it's like, if there's already something which exists, a building or in this case a jetty, that might look like something the same but bigger, then, nine times out of ten the planners and the government let it go ahead.'

'But why would that mean the Doss Tree is in danger?'

'It's because this is the flattest piece of land closest to the shore with no other vegetation other than the Doss tree and that overgrown vegetation over there. So, the factory part can be built on that site and the jetty can be expanded to bring the eels straight to it.'

'That's not fair,' shouted Megan, 'they can't cut down the Doss Tree' and she began to cry.

Shane told her to stop being a baby, although he agreed with her feelings.

'Yea? Why cut down the only tree in this field? Dolores surely the people can do something about it?'

'It's too late now. Before you came to live here lots of different people and environmental groups tried to stop the development but nothing seemed to work to change the minds of the people making the decisions. The lorry you saw yesterday brought the men who were to put the markers down for the building, surveying the site my mum called it. See the white pegs. That gives you an idea of the size of the building and as you can see we are nearly slap bang in the middle of their site.'

'Gosh it is big,' said Shane.

'Isn't it? It has been planned over the last five years. Even with all the protests, I mean everyone is against it, but the problem is, the lough shore is not owned by the people. Or the water for that matter. Yesterday was the start of it all beginning to finally happen!'

Everyone was quiet and no-one could think of anything to say.

Megan stepped forward and gave the tree a hug and closed her eyes.

Nathan laughed and said, 'Megan you're mad. Hugging a tree can't help it.'

'I don't care. Mum always says a hug can make horrible things go away 'cause you know you're loved.'

They all laughed and Shane suggested they join hands and give the tree a giant hug. By holding hands and pressing close to the tree they were able to encircle it. Shane was holding Dolores's right hand and everyone went very quiet.

Suddenly Dolores pulled her hands away from Shane and Megan.

'Who said that?'

'Who said what,' asked Shane.

'Someone asked me a question.'

'I didn't. Did you Nathan?'

'No. it must have been Megan.'

'I never did. I always get the blame,' and she began to sulk.

Dolores stepped away from the tree, 'I must go home now.'

The children were left wondering again about this strange girl.

'She really is a puzzle,' said Nathan

'Hmmm. She must have imagined it. We never heard any voices. Did we? Or was one of you messing about?'

Nathan and Megan protested their innocence and sat down beside the tree, both feeling hard done by.

'Maybe she's just in a mood? We'll catch her later. Let's go and find skimmers and see who can get the most skips across the water.'

They looked around for as many flat stones as they could find and spent the next twenty minutes trying to skip them across the calm waters of the lough. Shane won, but he always won. Nathan was closest with six and Megan could only manage a three for her top score. Feeling really annoyed now, because she hated being beaten by the boys at anything, she declared she was going to hug the Doss tree before going home for a drink.

She put her arms around the tree, closed her eyes and whispered 'Don't worry big Doss tree we'll look after you.'

Shane and Nathan Looked at their sister and were about to laugh when suddenly the central branch of the tree stirred and seemed to shake.

Shane looked at the water but it was perfectly calm.

Nathan said, 'Where did the wind come from?'

'I don't know – it's very odd!', Shane murmured, 'C'mon Nathan here's that lorry again. Let's go.'

'Look after me'

When the children had finished their dinner and were helping to clear things away Shane told his mum about what had happened at the tree.

'Very strange indeed. Did Megan say anything?'

'No, she just walked up home with us as if nothing had happened. Dolores was strange as well, going off like that and accusing us of saying something when none of us had.'

'She seems to be an unusual girl indeed, but the three of you like her, don't you?'

'We do but she always looks serious and rarely smiles.'

'Maybe it goes with the name.'

'What do you mean mum?'

'Well Dolores is a Spanish name and it means sorrows.'

'Gosh who would've thought that your name might reflect your personality.'

'No it doesn't really. I think your friend Dolores is very special as her mum told you. Maybe she worries about what that is and where she might fit in with her gift. It's very natural for everyone to wonder where their right place is in the world. Anyway why don't you nip down now and see her?'

'OK thanks mum.'

Shane found Dolores sitting on her swing at the back of the house.

'Hi there!'

'Hi.'

'Honestly none of us said anything today. We wouldn't mess you about. We want to be your friend.'

'I know, I'm sorry for walking off like that and you'll probably laugh at me, but if you or Nathan or Megan didn't say anything it .... it must have been the tree.'

'The tree! The Doss Tree!'

'See, I knew you'd laugh or not believe me. Forget it.'

'No, no, no. I do believe trees are living things. My dad told me a story once about a tribe of Indians in America. They would go into the forest to cut down a tree they needed, to make a canoe or a totem pole. The Medicine Man would pick the tree to be chopped down. Then what they did was they picked another tree and danced around it believing that all the other trees would think that they were safe. At the command of the Medicine Man they would pounce on the chosen tree and chop it down as quickly as possible. In that way they believed they were causing it as little pain as they could inflict on it.'

'That's a good story. I could believe that because sometimes I think the trees talk to each other particularly in a storm. When their branches get broken, it sounds as if they are in pain.'

'What did the tree say to you?'

'Promise you won't laugh?'

'I promise. Cross my heart and hope to die.'

'It said, 'Will you, look after me?''

'Look after me, hmmmm strange.'

Shane told what had happened when Megan hugged the tree earlier.

'Maybe it was her or maybe it was the arrival of the lorry again that made it shake with fear. It could have been a freak wind I suppose. But, maybe the Doss tree has magic after all and senses things. I don't know, but, maybe we should do something to protect it.'

'Like what?'

Shane sat on the grass and thought for a long while.

'Guerilla tactics that's what we need.'

'Gorilla tactics, what's that?'

'Not gorilla, grrrrrr, g,u,e,r, guerrilla tactics.'

'Well, what's that?'

'It's like when a bigger bad force from like a bigger country invades a smaller country, right. They can't fight on equal terms so they use cleverer tactics to undermine the big boys and make life really tough for them, in the hope they will get fed up and clear off.'

'That sounds good, but what can we do, we're only children?'

'I know, I know', Shane said despondently.

Dolores sat beside Shane on the grass. Both thought long and hard but no ideas seemed to appear.

Eventually Dolores said, 'let's go down to the Doss Tree and maybe we'll get the answer there?'

As they walked down the road, the lorry with the European flags approached. The driver and his passenger waved at them. They waved back, for both now realised they had to pretend they were friendly to hide anything they might get up to.

At the tree they saw there were more markers laid out and white lines were running between many of the markers.

Shane suddenly said, 'I know where we could make a start!'

'Don't say it. I know what you are going to say. Pull out the stakes and throw them in the lough.'

'How did you know?'

'I don't know. Maybe I just thought of it at the same time as you.'

'I don't know either. You seem to be able to hear things the rest of us don't and besides I didn't say it. Did I?'

'No. Anyway let's come down when it's getting dark and start our guerrilla campaign.'

'Yea, we could dress as Ninjas, so no one will see us in the dark.'

Dolores laughed.

'You have a nice laugh. You should laugh more often.'

'If we can save the Doss Tree I promise I'll laugh every day for the rest of my life.'

'That's a deal.'

They both touched the tree to seal their pact.

As they walked away the central branch of the Doss tree shook ever so slightly.

Let battle commence

Just after ten that night Shane said he was going to look at the stars. Nathan and Megan were already in bed reading.

'Put a jacket on in case it rains,' Shane's mum said.

'OK,' as he lifted his black raincoat.

Once outside he picked up Dolores who was standing by her hedge.'

'I see you're not dressed as a Ninja?'

Shane smiled.

'If I'd dressed up my parents would have got suspicious. I told them I was going stargazing.'

They both walked quietly down to the field and climbed over the metal gate.

'You go to the left of the Doss tree and I'll go right. We'll meet in the middle along the lough shore.'

'Good idea,' said Dolores as she pulled two heavy hammers out of a bag she was carrying.

'I thought the pegs could be quite difficult to pull out?' Hitting them on the sides should hopefully loosen them enough for us to pull them out.'

'Let battle commence,' Shane whispered loudly.

Using the last remaining glimmers of summer light they walked the white lines pulling the pegs free of the soil, sometimes having to use the hammers. By the time they met at the lough shore they had gathered two great bundles between them.

'I don't think we should throw them in the lough after all. They'll only float close to the shore. It would be different if there was a tide like at the seaside to carry them away.'

'Right,' said Dolores, 'tell you what. Bring them up to my house and we'll hide them in the wood shed. We'll cover them with some of the logs. No one will see them and there'll be no fires lit until late September or maybe October.'

When the pegs were hidden Shane needed to get home pretty quickly as he thought his Dad might by now be out looking for him.

'OK see you tomorrow.'

'Night 'Gorrilla Dolores',' he threw back as he ran up the road.

The next morning as the three children were having breakfast Shane whispered to Nathan and Megan, 'We're going to save the Doss Tree. Dolores and I have started a guerrilla war.'

Nathan laughed and said, 'you look nothing like a gorilla.'

Megan laughed.

'Look, seriously.'

Megan Looked at her brothers, 'That's funny. Yesterday when I hugged the tree before coming home, I said something to it and now you're going to help it. I told you hugs' work.'

'What did you say?'

'I told it we'd look after it, that's all.'

Shane looked at Nathan, 'Dolores told me that it must have been the tree that spoke to her because none of us said anything and it asked her to help it.'

'Perhaps the tree was responding after all and it wasn't the wind. The tree asked the question but instead of Dolores answering it, Megan answered instead. What do you think Nathan?'

'I don't know. Trees can't talk, can they? Maybe they only talk to girls,' he snorted.

'I don't know either but what if the Doss Tree is very special and because of that it is very important to this whole area. It holds the key to secrets about the Lough and maybe Dolores doesn't know it yet but she is the one to find the secrets out.'

Aunt Sally came in to the kitchen and told them to finish their breakfast and get out into the fresh air.

Nathan asked Shane about the guerrilla war but Shane told him the less he knew the less bother he would get into.

'I'll tell you sometime because we may need your help as well.'

When the police arrived in Doss in an unmarked car later that morning, it was Dolores who came bursting in to the kitchen.

'The police have arrived to inspect the site around the Doss Tree.'

Aunt Sally asked 'Why would the police need to inspect the site?'

'I, I don't know,' blurted out Dolores and looked at Shane, who quickly pretended he was Looking out the window at the lough.

'Very strange,' said Aunt Sally.

Shane then said rather nervously to deflect away from any further interrogation,

'Maybe they have found buried Viking treasure and the police have to guard it so that no one can steal it. All buried treasure belongs to the government, dad told me that.'

Aunt Sally looked at Shane, 'That, would be exciting, but it has nothing to do with us. I'm sure the police will take care of whatever it is.'

Dolores Looked at Shane and with her eyes indicated to him that they should go outside.

'Aunt Sally we'll go down to the lough shore and see what's happening. C'mon Nathan and Megan.'

With that they left the kitchen in double quick time.

Walking down the road Shane managed to whisper to Dolores that he had not told Nathan or Megan what they had done.

'You need to tell them,' she hissed back, 'we might need their help, because we might be in trouble already.'

'OK, OK, I'll tell them later.'

The men from the lorry were showing the police officers where they had put the pegs and telling them that someone must have sabotaged their site. One of the officers had his notebook out and was writing down the details. When they had finished they climbed over the gate to get in to their car. It was Dolores, who asked rather nervously,

'Excuse me officer, have they found buried treasure?'

The two policemen laughed, 'that certainly would have been more interesting. Nothing to concern you young lady or your friends. But perhaps you could tell us if you saw anything unusual last night.'

'You mean like ghosts or fish smugglers?' stammered Shane.

'No. Nothing like that, just somebody, making a bit of mischief for these men that are working here.'

They all shook their heads and Shane and Dolores managed to choke out 'No.'

'Well, if you hear anything tell your parents and they can get in touch with us at Randalstown Police Station.'

With that they got in the car and drove back up the Cargin Road.

The children stood and watched the workmen in the Doss Tree field. One of them was on his mobile phone talking rather loudly and saying that they needed new pegs right away as the excavator was to arrive the next day to begin digging.

Shane Looked at Dolores and both realised this was turning into something a lot bigger.

Rather forlornly they walked to Dolores' house. Megan got on the swing and asked Nathan to push her. Dolores and Shane sat on the grass looking decidedly worried. Nathan was watching them and asked, 'Was that part of your guerrilla campaign?'

It was Dolores who said, 'We need to talk. I didn't think the police would be called. My mum and Dad will kill me if they think that I was doing anything wrong.'

'Same here,' said Shane.

As Megan swung in the air, she shouted, 'Well I told the Doss Tree we would look after it, and it had already asked Dolores for help so it seems to me that what you're doing is right. Everything else has failed. Nobody got hurt, did they? And nobody else is doing anything anyway.'

Nathan stopped pushing Megan and sat down on the grass.

'Megan's right.' He looked at his big brother, and then at Dolores, 'You have a special gift and perhaps the Doss Tree is your way of finding out what that gift is. The tree responded to Megan, I now believe that. Maybe if you try to talk to it then it will help us find a way to save it.'

'Do you think so?'

Dolores looked quite scared.

Shane took her hand, 'Megan come off the swing and sit down with us.'

'Nathan hold Dolores' other hand and Megan hold my hand and Nathans'

The four children held hands. 'Now when we first all held hands and gave the Doss Tree a hug, Dolores heard the voice. We all agree that the tree was talking to Dolores, right?'

'Right,' the other three chorused.

'Well, I think this evening when the men have gone we go back and do the same thing and see if Dolores gets any new message. Agreed?'

'Agreed.' The other three nodded their heads.

'But what if our parents start asking questions, we'll be in trouble?'

'If the Doss Tree has special powers and is able to talk with you Dolores then I'm pretty sure it will look after us and we won't get into trouble with our parents, or the police. I'm beginning to think the Doss Tree knows things which have been lost to the people of Doss a long time ago - probably because this area has not faced danger for a long time.'

Everyone was quiet for a while and then Dolores said, 'Thank you for what you just said. I am afraid, but with you and your brother and sister I think I can help the Doss Tree. If you are all strong, I'll be strong. Tonight at nine o' clock we meet at the Doss Tree and we'll see what happens.'

Dolores' Mum appeared at the back door, 'Whatever are you lot up to?'

Quick as a flash Shane said with a grimace, 'Duuhh, caught playing Ring a Ring a Rosie with the girls.'

And they all burst out laughing.

Find the Queen

At nine o' clock the children climbed over the gate and approached the Doss Tree. They were all feeling a little nervous and it has to be said somewhat scared. Shane had been putting a brave face on it, but, he was feeling quite frightened even though he believed that Dolores did hold the key to unlocking the Doss Tree secrets.

Once again they circled the tree and joined hands. It was a beautiful calm evening with a red sky to the west. This time Dolores spoke directly to the tree. 'Doss Tree, are you trying to tell us something about how we can save you and keep this part of the lough from being destroyed?'

There was no response.

Just as Dolores was about to say to Shane, that this was a crazy idea, the large central branch of the tree stirred. The children stood shivering, holding hands and hugging the tree. Dolores closed her eyes and Shane could see she was nodding her head ever so slightly. After what seemed a long time she opened her eyes and smiled the biggest smile that just seemed to light up her whole face. Shane smiled, rather awkwardly back, but asked, 'Well, did anything happen?'

Dolores let go the hands of Shane and Nathan. 'C'mon sit down so I can I tell you the most amazing thing!'

Facing the other three children with her back against the tree, 'We have got a Queen!'

'I know that,' said Nathan rather sarcastically, 'she lives in Buckingham Palace in London.'

'No, no, no,' replied Dolores gleefully, 'we have a Queen of the Faeries.'

Megan almost shouted, 'Queen of the Faeries!'

'Yes, and she is the one who can save the Doss Tree.'

Shane looked intently at Dolores, 'You want us to believe there are faeries? That there is some Queen of the Faeries, who's going to come here and chase away diggers and builders and something that is called Corporate Europe? I don't think so.'

Dolores went quiet but Megan said to her brother, 'You never believe in anything, why shouldn't there be faeries? Mummy always says, there are strange things that happen in life and sometimes we just can't explain them.'

'Yea, but is that not what God does?' asked Nathan.

'Look, be quiet. Give me a chance to tell you what exactly the Doss Tree said to me. OK?'

'OK, go on,' said a very sceptical Shane.

'It first of all thanked us for coming back and for hugging it. It said to give Megan a special thank you for the hugging and for saying we would look after it.'

Megan made a face at her two brothers, as if to say, 'Nah, nah, nah, nah, nah.'

'There is a Queen of the Faeries but to get to her we have to complete three tasks. It seems she has hidden away from the world for so long that no-one knows where she is now, although the Doss Tree, I think, has an idea. Once we complete the three tasks the Faerie Queen should come and she will know what to do. The three tasks involve water, air and land and if we complete them correctly the Doss Tree says the Faerie Queen will let herself be known to us.'

'What if we don't get the tasks completed?' asked Shane

'I don't know, the Doss Tree never said.'

'So what is the first task?'

'Our first task is to take something that is really valuable to us or to one of us and offer it to the lough. The second task is to send a message to the air asking for the queen to help.'

'And, the last one?'

'To seek out the faerie thorn tree, at Cranfield Graveyard, which has not been seen for a hundred years, and, make it free.'

'I can see right away how easy it might be to do the first one but I'm not sure about the other two.'

Shane shook his head.

Nathan and Megan sat there looking totally baffled and Dolores was now rather dejected.

It was left to Shane to break the mood and he suggested that they all go home and sleep on it. Perhaps when they met up again tomorrow the way to move forward with the tasks would present itself.

'I agree, but we need to move quickly. You heard the diggers are coming and if they get to complete their work it will be impossible to change things.'

They left to go home and turning for a last Look at the tree all four instinctively reached out and touched the Doss Tree. The centre branch stirred in response and all four children felt as if a great weight had been lifted off them.

'The Doss Tree said everything will be all right,' and Dolores smiled her bright smile again.

When Shane finally went to bed he couldn't get to sleep and tossed and turned, thinking about the three tasks – earth, air and water – something precious, a message and finding the lost faerie tree. At around midnight he got out of bed and went to the kitchen for a glass of milk. His Mum was still working at her computer finishing a report.

'What's got you out of bed?'

'Oh nothing Mum.'

'You don't sound very convincing. What's wrong?'

Shane went to the fridge and got the milk and poured himself a glass.

'If I told you I know you won't believe me.'

'You could try me.'

After a while Shane told his Mum everything. When he finished his Mum scolded him about his 'guerilla attack' and the fact that the police were involved.

'What's your Dad going to say? Honestly I thought you had more sense.'

'Sorry Mum, but Dolores is really hurting over this whole business. I think everyone has let her down and now this area will never be the same again. You must admit it would be a shame to destroy that whole area around the Doss tree.'

'I don't disagree Shane, but you can't go interfering with men's work and not expect to suffer some consequences.'

Shane sat looking at his mother rather forlornly and seemed about to cry.

His Mum got up and gave him a hug, 'Finish your milk and get off to bed, you need your sleep. I'm off to bed as well'

As he turned at the door of the kitchen to say goodnight, he said to his Mum, 'but what about the Faerie Queen? If we could complete the three tasks maybe she will come and help? I'm not sure there is such a being, but Dolores was totally convinced. Listening to the tree made her really happy.'

'I'll think about your three tasks and have a chat with your Dad. I won't tell him about you interfering at the site. Just promise me, no more silly games. As for Faeries, maybe nature has a way of protecting itself and we just no longer understand it and give it other names from the past. Sometimes folklore and reality can be very close. Goodnight son.'

'Goodnight Mum. Thanks, and, thanks for not laughing at us.'

The next day the diggers never arrived. When the two men in the lorry came they only stayed a short while to check that the pegs and white lines were still in place. Dolores had watched all this from her house and when they left she immediately ran to tell Shane, Nathan and Megan.

'Maybe this is a sign that things will be OK?'

'I don't think so,' said Shane, 'anyway I told my Mum everything last night.'

'You what! I suppose she laughed at how silly we're all being.' Dolores turned to storm out of the kitchen.

'Wait Dolores, please,' pleaded Shane.

Dolores and his brother and sister stood looking at him for an explanation.

'Look, I couldn't sleep and Mum was up working late. She knew something was wrong so I told her. I couldn't lie to my Mum, could I?'

'Well you certainly tell plenty of fibs when it suits you,' said Nathan, and Megan nodded her head in agreement.

'Well this is different. This is very serious. It was the three tasks which I couldn't get my head round and if this Faerie Queen is out there, then we need a bit of help to get them sorted. Look, tomorrow's Saturday and Aunt Sally's away back home, so why don't you come round Dolores and we'll see if our Mum and Dad can come up with some ideas. OK?'

Three Tasks

Dolores arrived at the back door at exactly eleven o'clock the following morning and after knocking came in to the kitchen.

'Eleven o'clock, always a good time to start anything,' said Shane's Mum as she went to sit at the kitchen table.

'Shane, call Nathan and Megan in so that we can have our meeting.'

When they were all seated it was Shane's Mum who opened the discussion in a very light hearted way.

'Right, OK you lot, I believe that you are trying to save the Doss Tree. Dolores I've told their Dad what Shane has told me and we think that we can help you with your three tasks. The first one we think is the most difficult, because what is so precious to any of you that you would be prepared to sacrifice it to the water in the lough. So you will have to think really hard about that as the answer has to come from one of you four. The air message we think might be solved using a Sky lantern.'

'A Sky lantern? What's that?' asked Megan.

'It's a Chinese lantern made originally from rice paper on a bamboo frame so it is very light. You then attach some flammable material like a small candle to it, which makes it rise into the sky, you know like a mini hot air balloon. It will stay up as long as the flame burns. In Thailand it is considered good luck and many Thais believe their problems and worries float away with the lantern'

'Gosh,' said Dolores, 'do you think that will really work?'

'Well, we think it is your best chance to get a message into the air,' said Shane's Dad,' we need to make sure it is totally safe. At least we are not near any airports so there is no danger to aircraft. If the wind is right it could carry it out over the lough and then what's left when the flame burns out will drop down into the water. Everything has to be made from biodegradable materials so it won't harm the natural environment when it falls out of the sky – not even the fish in the lough.'

'What about the Faerie Thorn Tree at Cranfield Dad? We can't go digging around in a graveyard, can we?' Shane looked at his parents.

Both of them smiled.

'That my son was the easiest one of all to solve. I made a phone call to our local council offices in Antrim and had a chat with a friend of mine who works in the planning department and who oversees ancient sites. He called me back later and said that with very little investigation of the history of the Cranfield site he found the story of an ancient Faerie Thorn Tree near the old church. He was also able to tell me that, in talking to a couple of the councillors, a team of men are to be dispatched on Monday to begin clearing the overgrown part of the site. Maybe your Faerie Thorn will reveal itself. What do you think Dolores?'

Dolores just sat there and smiled.

It was Nathan who broke the silence, 'Does that mean if we complete all the tasks then the Faerie Queen will appear, just as Dolores told us would happen. Which means - the Doss Tree is very much alive and will be saved?'

'Now Nathan, your Dad and I are not promising that the Doss Tree will be saved and this big corporation will stop what they are doing. There does seem to be something happening here though. Dolores and you three appear to have tapped into whatever that is. We don't want you to get your hopes up, but, let's see what happens once the tasks are finished. Firstly, remember, something precious for the water and you'd better start making the lantern, and Dolores, you need to tell your Mum and Dad what's going on, OK?'

'OK, thankyou.' Dolores smiled her best smile and left.

After lunch Dolores had come back and told everyone that her Mum and Dad now knew everything, but didn't say she also got a strong scolding for interfering on the site around the Doss tree. She had gone to the tree after that and had something to tell them.

'I told the Doss Tree what we were doing and it said that things will happen very quickly. It was able to tell me that the reason the diggers have not arrived was the fact that the lorry which was to transport them had broken down. Amazing eh?'

'Maybe just a coincidence,' said Shane.

'Maybe. It also told me that if you send a message to the Faerie Queen you have to send it as a rhyme. Faeries it seems like poetry, rhymes, songs and everything musical.'

'Gosh, I'm no good at writing poetry. Megan you're always making up silly rhymes maybe you can think of something?'

'I don't know. This is too important. You'll all have to help me!'

'Of course we'll all help. Now let's make the lantern and whilst we're doing that we have to think of something really precious that we sacrifice to the lough.'

They sat round the table in the kitchen. Megan began scribbling on a sheet of paper. Their Mum had left a large square shaped lampshade to act as the template. Shane and Dolores started to measure out tissue paper and Nathan got out all the straws supplied for making a framework to attach the paper to. Dolores was good with her hands and Shane was always making things out of *Lego*. Together, with lots of patience, they worked out how to stick the straws together with glue. When this framework was finished it looked somewhat like a cage with an opening at the bottom.

'Right let that dry for a while before we attach the tissue paper. Megan, how's the rhyme coming on?'

'It's not very good and it doesn't rhyme.'

'Faerie Queen, Faerie Queen, too long unseen.

The Doss Tree's in danger, we need your help!'

'OK the first line is great but the second line has to rhyme.'

They all sat round the table looking at each other. Then Nathan said, 'Look we all believe that the Faerie Queen is out there, it's not just our imagination, right? So there has to be something about that.'

Again there was silence.

Eventually Dolores said very quietly,

'Faerie Queen, Faerie Queen, too long unseen.

We know you exist, you're not just a dream.'

'That's it, brilliant. We can add a PS which says the Doss Tree's in danger. Now let's write that very carefully on part of our tissue paper to go on the lantern,' said Shane excitedly.

'We all have to sign it as well,' said Nathan.

'OK, Dolores you write the rhyme, sign it, then we all sign it and then you add the PS, agreed?

Everyone agreed and by the time this was finished the straw framework was firmly stuck together. Eight lines of sewing thread were attached to the bottom part of the framework trailing down to be tied to eight tiny holes at the top of a little cardboard basket which would carry the nightlight candle below the lantern.

When their Mum arrived home from doing the shopping she congratulated them on their great work, but asked why they were still looking so glum.

'We can't think of something that is precious enough to sacrifice to the lough,' said Shane, 'Nathan said he would give up his teddy bear but we all think that's not good enough. Megan would give up her favourite *SPONGEBOB* DVD, but, again we all think that's no good either. I just can't think of anything that is really precious to me and Dolores hasn't said anything.'

'Perhaps Dolores knows the answer but is a little afraid to tell you all?' said Shane's Mum.

'Is that true?' asked Shane in a concerned voice.

'Yes. I think I have the answer but I need to go home and talk to my Mum and Dad. Is that OK?'

'Of course,' said Shane, 'and if you decide it's all right and your Mum and Dad agree then we could do the first two tasks this evening just as it's getting dark and our parents can be there to watch.'

Dolores stood there for a second as if uncertain, gave a weak smile, turned and left the kitchen without another word.

A strange fire

It turned out that what was really precious for Dolores, were the ashes of her dog Jack. Not long after she was born her Dad had gone to the animal sanctuary, and there newly arrived were five cuddly black cross retriever pups. He picked one with enormous paws and brought him home. Jack grew to be a really big dog. Everyone agreed there must be Newfoundlander in him. Apart from his huge size the main trait of his nature was gentleness. All Dolores' sisters played with Jack but he had a special feeling for Dolores and went everywhere with her, protecting her as she grew up. He had only died the year before and the family had Jack cremated. When his ashes were brought home Dolores put them in the leather pouch in which she used to carry Jack's treats. The pouch sat on the dressing table in her bedroom next to the spot where Jack had slept at night.

With torches aglow in the dark, the two families stood at the end of the jetty watching Dolores pour Jack's ashes into the waters of the Lough. For a while she stood there seemingly frozen to the spot. Eventually her Dad stepped forward and giving her a hug said, 'Well done, now let's light this lantern.'
Straightening her shoulders she turned and faced her family and her new friends. Shane was holding the lantern and stepped forward, 'You've got the matches. Light the candle.'

Once the candle was lit both Shane and Dolores held the lantern very lightly until as if by magic the warm air inside the lantern gently lifted it from their fingers and carried it into the darkness of the night. It kept rising and rising heading towards Ballyronan on the other side of the lough.

Everyone was silent.

Suddenly the Doss Tree seemed to stir and the central branch started to move.

No one realised until Nathan shouted out, 'The lantern is changing direction!'

As the lantern came back towards them their eyes tracked its path above the Doss Tree and everyone could now see, with the help of the moon, that the central branch was swaying.

'The Doss Tree made it change direction,' said Shane.

'Don't be daft son. It's just the wind changing,' said his dad.

'Yes, it happens down here at Doss. One minute the wind can be blowing from the north and the next it can shift to be coming from the east,' said Dolores' Dad.

'But Dad the wind was behind us tonight, you said that it was coming from the east so it would be safe to launch the lantern away from the direction of the airport. Now it's going towards the airport and coming from the west.'

'I hope this doesn't mean that this part is going to go wrong and that means the Faerie Queen is not going to appear,' wailed Megan.

'Stop that now Megan. You've all done your best and the council will do the rest on Monday. It's not over yet.'

Dolores' Mum invited everyone up to their house for supper and as they turned to go Shane said to Dolores, 'What if Megan's right? The Doss Tree did say the three tasks had to be completed correctly for it to work. We're not finding the Faerie Thorn tree and now our message seems to be going in a different direction?'

'I don't think it is. The strength of the Doss Tree is only beginning to show itself,' and Dolores gave Shane a playful tap on his arm.

Meanwhile across the lough at Cranfield the local people were enjoying a quiet drink in the Cranfield Arms. Established in 1873 traditionally there was music in the pub on a Saturday night but on this particular night there was no band. A couple of the smokers were standing outside chatting when one of them pointed to the sky.

'What's that?'

The other looked skywards and started to laugh.

'Maybe it's one of those UFOs you hear about?'

They both laughed and putting out their cigarettes went back into the bar.

If they had waited a little while longer they would have seen their 'UFO' land in the graveyard. After a few minutes there was a loud whoosh sound and a brightness appeared at the place where it had landed. The brightness died away and a faint smokey smell drifted towards the pub. Nobody passed any remark about this smell as everyone assumed it was the remaining passive smoke left by the smokers.

On Monday morning when the council workers appeared to clear the site at the graveyard they found the ground at the corner close to the old church burnt black.

In the centre of this black area, stood a hawthorn bush, with hardly a mark on it!

When they reported back to the man who was the friend of Shane's Dad they said there must have been some kind of strange fire in the graveyard. When asked to explain they said everything in what they had been told was the overgrown part had been burnt away except for the hawthorn bush.

It was dismissed as a freak accident perhaps started by someone's carelessness and anyway hawthorn bushes are notoriously tough. By the time it might have caught fire the rest of the overgrown bushes had perhaps already burnt out.

That night when Shane's dad got home from work he told them what his friend in the council had said. The three children sat listening in silence and after their Dad had finished, without saying a word, they got up, left the house, and ran down the road to Dolores' house.

They burst through the back door without knocking and to the astonishment of Dolores' Mum and Dad blurted out the story of the fire. Then Shane asked, 'Do you think the lantern started the fire to free the Faerie Thorn? It did go in that direction.'

Dolores' Dad said that it could be the biggest coincidence he'd ever heard of and laughed heartily.

Dolores turned to her Dad, 'Dad I need to go to the Doss Tree with my friends. Is that all right?'

He smiled at her, 'You go to the tree my lovely. You haven't been out of the house since you put Jack's ashes in the lough.'

Once again the children held hands and hugged the tree.

Once again the central branch began to stir.

Once again Dolores closed her eyes.

Once again her head began to nod in answer to the Doss Tree.

A gathering of armies

They stood holding hands long after Dolores had stopped nodding her head. They seemed to be gaining great peace and strength from being so close to the tree. Finally Dolores opened her eyes and said everything would happen in the next few days.

'The Faerie Queen is free and is presently flying above us, on a buzzard, familiarising herself with this landscape again. It seems Faeries can only fly to a certain height, so when they want a really high perspective they use raptor birds like the Common Buzzard that are plentiful in this area. She is also visiting all the Faerie kingdoms which are found along this part of the lough shore. The Queen will be working hard to convince all the other Faeries that the Doss Tree and the surrounding area needs to be saved. If she is successful, the Doss Tree says there will be a gathering of armies, or Faerie Hosts, which should help to stop the building work.'

'What sort of armies are they?' asked Megan.

'The hidden Faerie armies, of the ancient Lough Kingdoms. Nobody has seen them for a long, long time.'

'But why do the Faeries need convincing that the Doss Tree and this beautiful area should be saved?' asked Shane.

'Well it seems the Faeries don't believe that we humans, what they call the People, want to protect not just this environment but many others. They think that all we want to do is to destroy natural environments to make money. They believe we don't really appreciate the Doss Tree and unless something drastic happens the tree will be sacrificed.'

'But <u>we</u> appreciate the Doss Tree,' shouted Nathan.

'Yes the Queen knows that and she is using us as part of her arguments. What we have done so far has been a statement of our intention and commitment, but,' and here she hesitated, 'that might not be enough,' and shook her head.

'Not enough,' said Shane, 'we nearly got into trouble with the police, we sent the message and by accident or design the Faerie Thorn at Cranfield is now free for all to see, and you Dolores you gave up the ashes of your favourite dog. All of that should convince them that we at least love the Doss Tree and this area. Should it not? And you, you were confident that the Doss Tree would make it all happen!'

'I don't know. Honest. The Doss Tree did say it will all work out. It is also partly why the Queen is flying so high, she is looking for something else that might save the tree if the armies are not strong enough to beat Corporate Europe. Faeries don't really have magical powers. It's just them and their environment, which they love deeply because it protects them and keeps them safe.'

'Something else, I wonder what that is,' murmured Shane.

Dolores hesitated for a while and then said, 'The Doss Tree told me that the Queen, like itself, has been waiting a long time for someone like me.'

The three stood looking at Dolores.

'We knew you were different,' smiled Nathan.

'Yes I now believe I am. But the Doss Tree told me, that my being different draws its strength from you my friends and my family. This gift of communicating with nature I'm told is in all of us. We have forgotten how to do it. We just need to re-learn how to. It seems I'm lucky being the seventh daughter of a seventh daughter. It places me in a unique position. I think I might just be extra sensitive and more aware of the importance of all living things. Not just people.'

'That sounds like an awful lot of responsibility.'

Shane looked at his friend rather intently as if he was seeing her for the first time.

Dolores gave the three of them her biggest smile. 'No. Not really. Remember, I've got you, your family and mine to share my 'awful lot of responsibility'. Now let's go back up to the house and see what happens next.'

'Before we go,' said Megan, 'can you tell us what the Doss Tree sounds like?'

'Well I don't know, really, how to describe it. I guess it might be like listening to your favourite Grandad reading you a bedtime story and just as your drifting off to sleep feeling safe and warm his voice is like…, coming from a distance…, steady, strong, interesting - loving.'

Megan mulled that over for some time, 'I like that. I can understand that. Thanks Dolores.'

Before they left the field all four touched the tree.

As they walked away the tree responded with a rustle of the leaves on its middle branch.

Not far away from Doss Point, on the *Skady Tower*, a little island off the shoreline, the Queen was in discussions with the leaders of the Faerie Hosts. These leaders had been elected from all the Faeries in their clan because they had demonstrated the main qualities required for leading each Faerie kingdom in times of trouble. After the speeches and the discussions around tactics, decisions were made. The Queen was then tasked with delivering this information to the one human who would understand their role in helping to save the Doss Tree and the surrounding area.

A dream

Dolores had slept fitfully that night and had awakened in the early hours with the strange feeling that someone had been talking to her.

Everything was quiet.

Dolores thought it had been a dream, but, there was now so much stuff in her head about the Faeries and what they were going to do. Dolores knew it couldn't have been a dream. She got out of bed and went to the window to look at the Doss Tree. She was certain that a small bright light was sitting at the top of the centre branch of the Doss Tree. The tree was gently swaying in the moonlight. After a while the light took off towards the lough shore and disappeared. When the tree stopped swaying Dolores got back into bed and after going over everything in her head again, fell asleep.

When she awoke in the morning it was all still there. She couldn't wait to tell her friends all about the Faerie Folk.

'But what if it was only a dream?' asked Shane rather sceptically.

'No. I'm totally convinced I was spoken to by the Queen during the night. Wait until you hear what I have to say and then you can judge. OK?'

Shane nodded.

Megan glared at her older brother.

'There are five Faerie kingdoms that cover this part of the Lough Neagh shoreline and they are the ones who would lose the most if Corporate Europe wins. In the olden days their names were very different and their boundaries were marked by special stones with strange marks on them. These marks were called by us, *Ogham,* named after an Irish god called Ogma. So that we can find where their kingdoms roughly are I was given their modern names which come from the bays around the shore, *Brockish* close to Toome, *Doss* where we are, *Pollan, Gawleys* and the biggest kingdom which is *Cranfield.* Cranfield is where the Queen resides. Every kingdom is independent but the Queen's role in times of trouble is to pull everyone together for the good of all.'

Shane held up his hands, 'So why was she having such trouble getting them all to help?'

'Let her tell the story Shane, pleeeease,' said Nathan.

'Sorry, go on.'

'The Brockish Faeries are called the Bards because they love poetry and music. Doss Faeries have the title Devils for they are always doing bad things to other Faeries and it seems create mischief for us humans. The Pollan Faeries are really small and so are called Pygmies whilst the Gawleys' Faeries are called Giants because of their size compared to other Faeries, but to us are still very, very small. The Cranfield Faeries are called the Reds because of the colour of their hair and the beards of the males.'

'I thought we were the only ones who gave nicknames to people and things,' said Shane.

'It might be the other way around. The Faerie Folk have done it for thousands of years. In the past we learned it from them, but, like a lot of things we have forgotten where they originated. Anyway, the first thing the Faeries did in their own kingdoms was to call a war council. At that war council they elected their war chief who would then go forward to meet with the Queen and argue their case for fighting or not. The Faerie that gets chosen is usually one who is outstanding in their kingdom and must be at least brave, but must most of all, have the good of their kingdom and all Faerie kingdoms burning in their heart. At that meeting the Queen gives them a new name chosen by her to carry the battle to the enemy. She also awards them their colour to fight under.'

Nathan put his hand up as if in school, 'excuse me, it all sounds very complicated?'

'No, no, not really. Wait till I tell you what happens next and then it may make sense. The five chosen leaders arrived at the Skady Tower island where Faeries have been holding meetings for thousands of years and before the discussions took place the Queen gave them their new names and colours.'

The Queen sat on her throne carved from bog oak which had been buried for 7,000 years in the great blanket bog of the Antrim Plateau. The golden hair of the Queen and her lime green flowing robes were in stark contrast to the jet black of her ceremonial throne. Before her in a semi-circle were placed five emerald green velvet seats. Behind them, stood the chosen five leaders from the Five Kingdoms of the north eastern shore of Lough Neagh. The Queen cast her eyes over the five before she spoke.

'Tadhg the Poet, step forward and take your seat at this council. I name you Aimhirghin, born of song, to uphold the strength of the Brockish Kingdom and I confer on you the colour black to carry into battle if that is your wish.'

'I thank the Queen for this great honour and in the debate that is to come I will do my best to keep the concerns of our Faerie kingdoms to the fore.'

Aimhirghin bowed and sat down.

'I recognise Treasach the Fierce of the Doss Devils. I name you Breasal, the Brave, and I give you the colour brown in the hope that it might curb your nature and help you to support the good of all Faerie Folk.'

'I thank the Queen for this honour. My nature is that of my folk and that I will always bring to any debate and battle, if it comes.'

Breasal bowed and sat down.

'Ruarc the Champion of the Pollan Pygmies come forth. I name you Conall, strong as a wolf, and I bestow on you the colour purple for your flags and battle shirts.'

'I thank the Queen for this great honour. As you know my Queen we pygmies are always forthright in our discussions.'

Conall bowed, stood up and drawing himself as tall as he could, took his place.

Tuathla the Princess of the Gawleys Giants was called next.

The Queen smiled, 'I name you Saraid, the best, for you are most excellent of your folk. I recognise the strength of your sisters and your brothers. For that I award you the colour gold.'

The tallest of the Faeries stepped forward, bowed and with the most graceful of movement took her seat.

Lastly Aodh the Firebrand of the Cranfield Reds was called forward.

The Queen Looked at Aodh and knew that he would be the toughest one to sway in favour of the Doss Tree when it came to the debate. Before giving him his name she had thought very carefully.

'Aodh the Firebrand, I name you Fiachra, battle king.'

This indeed was a singular honour and the other leaders stiffened slightly at the title 'king', but having accepted their seat on the council they could not now object to this last conferment.

'Your colour is green and I welcome you to this important council which hereafter will be referred to as the The Doss Tree Council.'

Very stiffly Fiachra bowed and without acknowledging the other four leaders took the final seat on the council.

The Queen stood up to set in motion the debate which was to take place.

'My generals you have been chosen by your Folk to bring forward their views and concerns. The decision to fight for the Doss Tree and its land rests with you. There are five of you as battle leaders and I as your queen make six. We are all equal when it comes to deciding our course but in the event of a tied vote I remind you that I carry an extra vote in my position as Queen. In that event I hope you will trust me to make the right decision. Now who wishes to open our Doss Tree Council.'

There was silence for a moment until Conall stood up and took the floor.

'My Queen you have given me the name 'strong as a wolf' because you have recognised how I am held amongst my Folk. I am not given to great thoughts or debate but I do believe that actions speak louder than words. The Doss Tree is in danger and if we are to safeguard the most ancient of the last great trees on this island then we must act. To me it is simple, we must do all that we can. What we should be doing now is discussing our tactics and not whether or not we should be doing anything at all.'

With that he sat down.

'The Queen recognises Aimhirghin.'

'I thank my Queen.'

Aimhirghin looked directly at the other four leaders, 'The first time we were pushed away from the People was when Druids came into our world and wanted the power over them for themselves. Until that time we had lived in total harmony with the People. They recognised our strengths and accepted us for what we were. We lived harmoniously with the land, the water and the air and we did not seek to dominate anything or anyone. Once the Druids became influential, time began to play a role with new generations of the People. Gradually they forgot about us. The People didn't feel the need to defer to us and began to exploit the land, the water and the air, never mind what the consequences might be. We have seen what has happened over the years. Our beautiful lough has been polluted so many times, fish die in the rivers, birdsong is disappearing with the destruction of the hedgerows and there is so much smoke in the air at times that we all have difficulty breathing. You ask me to support the saving of the Doss tree…….. I say it is already a lost cause.' He sat down.

Immediately Breasal took the floor.

'My courage is not under question but I concur with Aimhirghin my Queen. All that he says is true. The People do not deserve to look after the beauty that they live with. I would also add, what can be done against the monstrous machines which they will send to destroy the Doss Tree.'

Silence descended on the Council.

Saraid's dulcet voice broke the silence.

'My Queen I understand that among the People has come one who understands and can commune with the great heritage of living things?'

'Yes this is true. Her name is Dolores and with her friends she has opened an important avenue of communication with the Doss Tree. She understands why it is important to fight for living things……. including us.'

Saraid's voice softened, 'Perhaps we should take hope in this Dolores. Is she not worth fighting for my fellow leaders?'

Again there was silence until Fiachra's voice came in bitter and hard.

'My Queen, I don't care for any of the People. They are deceitful. They will tell you one thing and go and do the complete opposite, they always have. Never mind the place where we exist, they do not care for their own kind who live in difficult circumstances in different parts of our world. I say, let them sort things out for themselves. Let us do what we have done since the time of the Druids, keep to ourselves and look after our own. We do not need to do anything for the People even if a special one has appeared.'

'The special one as you call her is worth fighting for as Saraid has said. For hundreds of years we have mourned the fact that the People have forgotten us and did not want to engage with our ways. The Doss Tree has made the most important connection for centuries. Through this human child it could be a new beginning. Perhaps in the past we too were arrogant about our position in this world. Maybe this is a chance for all of us to show that finally the balance between ourselves and the People will return to some kind of harmony. We now have a human connection to the greater world and without exposing ourselves we could ensure that the future will be better for all kinds that come after, even if we disappeared.'

This time Fiachra stood up and bowed.

'My Queen your argument is compelling but collectively our experiences tell me that we will be disappointed. I would like to believe like you that we could return to the great days when Faeries and People managed our world together. My final word on this matter is that our time for meddling in People affairs is long in the past, and that is where it should stay.'

A sombre mood descended on the Council until finally the Queen said.

'I will not ask you to do anything I would not do myself, nor place yourselves in danger, where I would not place myself. I will say this, Dolores is remarkable and if we miss this opportunity to show her what we can do for the beloved Doss Tree the Faerie Folk of Lough Neagh will disappear forever and life for the People will go on and we might as well never have existed. The Doss Tree trusts these children. It asked for help and they responded. It is not as old as us but I believe it has shown great wisdom. It too is prepared to place itself in danger if our efforts require help.'

'What danger can the Doss Tree place itself in?' asked Fiachra rather stiffly.

'I do not know. Only time will know. That time is running out very quickly. Fiachra, it is already in the greatest danger. The machines that Breasal mentioned will be here the day after tomorrow and if we do decide now to help then it might not be too late. Let us take a little time out and then put this Council to a vote.'

'My Queen,' Aimhirghin rose from his velvet seat, 'I spoke earlier against becoming involved, we do not need time out, the vote should be taken now. I have listened to everything that has been said and in particular about this young human, Dolores. I have sorely missed the music of the People and the contact we had in the past. I would welcome the chance again to bridge the chasm that opened up between us and the People. I have not changed my mind. I vote no.'

'Thankyou Aimhirghin. Breasal what say you?'

'I still believe this will be too destructive for our Folk. I vote no.' Breasal sat down with a heavy heart.

'What does Conall say?'

'As I said before my Queen it's time to talk tactics. I vote yes.'

'Fiachra of the Cranfield Reds, do you still say it will be wrong for us, that we should leave the People to themselves?'

'It's good to see that the Brockish Bards are now thinking with their heads and not their hearts. And as for you Pygmies, you are forever jumping into situations without thinking things through.'

'I would remind Fiachra,' said the Queen sternly, 'that there is no need to cast what would be considered negative comments on the other leaders. We are all equal here. I take it your vote is no? That is all I need for you to say.'

'My vote is no.'

'Saraid, your vote please, as the last member of the five. Then I will cast my vote.'

'The vote for the Gawleys' Faeries is yes. We will stand by the Doss Tree.'

'My thanks to all of you. This leaves the nos at three and the yes vote at two, which means ...'

Fiachra jumped up. 'My Queen you reside in our kingdom and you know how vital it is that we have no contact with this generation of People. They are I feel a lost People. I beg you to vote no. If you vote yes I know you will use your casting vote to say yes. If you do this thing we will lose everything. I do not trust the People, even this Dolores.'

The Queen was taken aback by this outburst and sat back on her throne looking at the Faerie she had named Fiachra, battle king. She had hoped that this greatest of honours which this name brought would have swayed him to her cause without her having to play the lead role. She had known all along how he would vote because of the way the People neglected the Cranfield area. As she was about to answer, Breasal rose to his feet.

'I recognise Breasal of the Doss Devils. You have the floor.'

'My Queen, my fellow leaders, I have not done justice to Dolores and her valiant friends. We have watched, in our way, these new friends of Dolores since they came into our kingdom. These are generous People, generous, not just to their own kind, but, generous to everything that is around them. They do care what happens. They have felt powerless against those who would seek to change an important part of our kingdom. My folk have said to me that we should support them. I have allowed my anger to cloud my own thinking, particularly the way the older People in power steamroll over everything to get their way. We love the Doss Tree. We love what it brings to our kingdom and it has been part of us for a long time. I'm not convinced we can beat the machines but I would never forgive myself if we didn't try and my Folk would not forgive me for not fighting back. If it is permissible my Queen I change my vote to yes. Yes to protect the Doss Tree.'

'This is an open discussion, you can change your mind. I think that means there is majority for yes, without my vote. Yes?'

Everyone nodded.

'Let us now begin to plan our tactics before it is too late. Fiachra I take it you are now with us?'

Fiachra stood, bowed to his Queen, turned and bowed to his fellow leaders and simply nodded his head once.

A victory

Shane burst into Dolores' kitchen. He had run all the way from his house. He managed to gasp out.

'The big diggers have arrived on the back of two lorries. They've turned into the field where the Doss Tree is!'

'Well, there is nothing that we can do now,' Dolores said calmly, 'we'll just have to wait and see if the plans that were made on Skady Tower will work. I have every faith in the Queen and the Faerie Hosts. Don't worry Shane, between the Queen and the Doss Tree I know things will be all right.'

Shane stood there breathing heavily but his mind was in turmoil because a large part of him thought that the battle to save the Doss Tree was already well and truly lost. He knew though that if he gave voice to his doubts he would lose the friendship of this remarkable girl and he didn't want that.

Silently he sat on one of the kitchen chairs.

It was Dolores' Mum who said, 'Looks as if the arrival of the diggers has created a bit of a stir. A crowd of your friends and our neighbours have gathered.'

Shane looked at Dolores. Both of them thought the same thing, diggers are nothing new in this part of the country. Why would any of them come to see diggers working?

This time it was Megan who ran into the kitchen.

Mrs Downey was about to say something when Megan shouted, 'come quick, come quick, something's happening!'

They all rushed out to where the small crowd were standing at the end of the slip road to the jetty.

In the distance towards Brockish Bay a dark cloud was approaching Doss Bay. As it got to Doss the cloud was getting much bigger.

Everyone, except Dolores, Shane, Nathan, Megan, and Dolores' mum were shouting, 'Look at the size of that swarm of flies!', 'never seen anything like it, in all my life!', 'o my gosh that's the worst May Fly swarm ever seen!', 'we'ed all better get away before they tangle in our ears and eyes!'

As they all left to go, Dolores, Shane, Nathan, Megan and Dolores' mum all swapped looks with one another and without saying anything stood together to watch what was about to unfold.

This was the first wave, the beginning of the Queen and her generals' plan.

The men were busy offloading the diggers and had not taken much notice of the approaching swarm. They could not hear the approach because of the sound of the diesel engines but Dolores could feel the intensity of the Faerie Hosts sound. It was like a giant murmuring host of people, but soft, as they encouraged one another not to be afraid.

No Faerie Host had ever tackled such machinery before.

Dolores closed her eyes and reached out to touch the hands of her friends.

'Aimhirghin and Breasal have now joined their Hosts together and they lead them from the front. Their aim is very simple to make a great nuisance of themselves, so that the men find it difficult to work.'

As she opened her eyes the swarm was now right on top of the men. From where they were standing the men looked like human windmills as they tried to swat the swarm away.

One of the men lifted a spade and was swinging it madly like a weapon. Another man who was in the cab of the digger jumped out. The cab had become totally engulfed. The man who was in charge shouted to the rest to leave everything for the moment and take refuge in the breeze block hut that had been built to house tools.

Megan was giggling and Nathan was busy shouting, 'c'mon the Doss Devils and give it to them the Brockish Bards!'

Dolores' mum was laughing and Shane and Dolores just stood there smiling.

The swarm settled over the diggers.

Eventually the men came out of the hut and there was much discussion as they stood and watched the 'black cloud' spectacle.

Breasal had dispatched one of his Devils to overhear what they were talking about. When he returned it was to say that the men couldn't work in those conditions and they would have to lock up the diggers and come back tomorrow.

'They think Mayfly swarms only last for short bursts.'

Aimhirghin who was party to this feedback suggested they keep hovering, even when they come to lock their cabs. That way they won't be tempted to start them up again, or think that we will be dispersing.

Breasal agreed, 'We have fought well today, a victory. We have lost many of our brothers and sisters. They have gone, been absorbed by Mother Earth. But, these People will soon realise that we are here to stay. We are not going anywhere.'

After the men had left, the swarm lifted off and part of it was seen heading towards the north.

Dolores with her friends walked over to the Doss Tree and this time they didn't have to hug it. Dolores leaned against the tree and closed her eyes. Her three friends waited until she was ready.

'The Doss Tree tells me there was a high price to pay for winning today. Many of the Faeries were hurt and were carried off. Many more were destroyed and when that happens the earth just absorbs them back into the soil. Some of the really brave ones who are outstanding in battle, and become destroyed, may come back in the form of a human. They become People like us and continue the fight to protect all living things.'

'You mean there could be Faeries walking around and we don't even know it?' said Nathan.

'The way the Doss Tree described it was, People with a fierce protective sense towards our environment. The Doss Tree also said that the People will be coming armed with their own tactics tomorrow and it might be the decisive day.'

'You mean it might be all over tomorrow?' asked Shane.

'I don't know, maybe?'

'We'll win,' said Megan, 'I just know we will.'

Everyone smiled.

The Doss Tree shook his middle branch and the leaves seem to whisper yessssssss.

Summon the Reds

Everyone woke early the next morning and were gathered in front of Dolores' house when the workmen arrived. Some of the other children in the area eventually turned up and stood where the lane turned down towards the jetty. Some of the men had arrived in a car but another had arrived with a lorry. Once they had all disembarked they went straight to the lorry where the tailboard was dropped to reveal a lot of metal barrels.

A digger was started.

Two of the men climbed on the back of the lorry and they rolled one of the barrels upright to the edge of the lorry. The digger was driven to the back of the lorry and the bucket was lifted to the edge of the lorry back. The two men rolled the first barrel on to the bucket of the digger. The digger driver was then directed to place it at a particular spot on the designated outline of the proposed factory.

There were twenty barrels lifted off.

Dolores and everyone else wondered,' what's with all these barrels?'

From the north again came the dark cloud. The Hosts of the Brockish and Doss kingdoms arrived with more mischief to commit among the men sent from Corporate Europe. As the cloud began to descend on the machinery a command was shouted by the manager of the Corporate Europe team.

'Light the barrels!'

The men took out matches, lit them, and, began dropping them into the barrels. Immediately, black smoke and flames started to belch out, leaving an oily smell in the air.

Dolores stood there absolutely shocked.

No one said a word.

The black smoke billowed into the air.

The swarm seemed to stop, and then, part of it began to descend towards the diggers.

Two of the men now started petrol driven leaf blowers.

Using the blowers they directed the oily smoke towards the dark swarm.

Aimirghin and Breasal who were leading the Hosts of Brockish and Doss were the first to be caught by the oily smoke. Choking as if it was their last breath they just managed to fly above and away from the poisonous particles being spewed from the barrels.

Thousands of their Hosts were not as quick, and, not as lucky.

The ground became littered with their remains before being taken to Mother Earth.

The Queen sat on her favourite buzzard, Miach the proud, and watched this serious setback. The Queen knew it was time to bring in the Pygmies and the Giants. The Bards and the Devils, were clearly not going to be a match for these People.

Miach was prompted to send messages to the Pollan and Gawleys kingdoms. With its high pitched shreeeek way of communicating, which only Faeries can understand, Conall and Saraid were called.

Their Faerie Hosts came together in no time at all.

From the south approached another great black cloud. The People of Doss swore afterwards that this swarm of flies was the most massive ever seen in the history of the Lough Neagh shores. Many of the farmers out cutting their silage had thought that an eclipse of the sun had taken place, so dark was the sky as the two great Hosts from Gawleys and Pollan moved to save the Doss Tree. Some of the farmers swore there were flashes of gold through the cloud as it passed, but put it down to rays of sunlight cutting through the cloud.

When Conall and Saraid arrived at Doss they saw the smoking barrels and the remainder of the Hosts from Brockish and Doss standing off to the north. The Queen swept out of the sky, with Miach, to meet with Conall and Saraid.

'My generals, I do not want you to be destroyed by this poison. The Hosts of Doss and Brockish are nearly through. Let us take a little time to see if there is another way to tackle this evil.'

The men from Corporate Europe, in keeping an eye on the sky, had now spotted this new cloud and wondered why it hovered not far from Doss Point. A buzzard was also spotted, flying above the cloud.

Saraid summoned her best captain, Fearghal the Valorous.

'Will you undertake a dangerous mission on behalf of your Folk and all the Faerie Folk of the North Eastern Kingdoms of the Lough?'

'My General, I thank you for the honour of choosing me, and yes, I will do whatever you ask of me, for the good of the North Eastern Kingdoms!'

'Feargal as you can see, the Doss tree is surrounded by toxic smoke. Toxic smoke that is dangerous for our kind. The People that have produced this think that we will be repelled. I ask that you fly down, please try and avoid the smoke, and see if there is a way that we can continue to interfere with these people and stop their progress.'

'My General, I will do my best.'

With that Fearghal left.

Saraid, Conall and the Queen waited until his return.

'My General, my Queen,' Fearghal coughed, 'I have done as you asked,' he coughed again. 'The only way to gain entry where the machines are and stop them working is, to fly across the Lough, turn and approach from the direction of Ballyronan, very, very low.' Fearghal coughed, 'Smoke will always rise because it is warm. Whatever substance they are using in the barrels may now begin to burn out. The blowing machines only work in one direction and if our Hosts can be careful they may avoid the worst. This way you can still get into their machinery, and amongst them.'

Fearghal went into a spasm of coughing. When he recovered he said, 'I fear though there will still be many casualties my General amongst our Folk, the smoke is fearsome.'

Fearghal's wings folded, he collapsed. Spiralling earthwards his Faerie form began to disintegrate and by the time it touched the Earth the particles that made up Fearghal were ready to become part of the soil.

The Queen Looked at Saraid and Conall. 'Neither the Doss Tree nor I foresaw this poisonous smoke. I fear we may lose many, many more of our great Faerie Hosts. The Doss Tree tells me it feels that the price is already too high. It is prepared to sacrifice itself for the sake of the remaining Hosts. It may be that in the world of today our ways are now finished. If you decide to call off your attack I will understand.'

'My Queen, we gave an undertaking to try and save the Doss Tree. If Conall is still of the same mind, like myself, I suggest we try what the valiant Fearghal suggested.'

The Queen bowed to Saraid and said simply. 'Thankyou.'

As Saraid and Conall were about to command their hosts, Breasal arrived.

'My Queen, my fellow generals, it is good that you have come to our aid for I feel we have failed miserably. I have come to warn you that they have more of that toxic substance and have begun adding it to the barrels. If you look now you can see more smoke pouring from the barrels. The People have also donned special safety helmets to protect them from the smoke and from us. I fear we must abandon our nuisance tactics.'

The Queen answered, 'It is time to summon the Cranfield Reds, but, they shall come armed with their stingers! Stingers made from the thorns of the toughest Hawthorn bushes'.

'My Queen, forgive me but part of our Faerie Code is not to do harm or bring hurt to others.'

For a long moment the Queen looked at Saraid.

In a hard voice which none of the Generals had heard from their Queen, she replied, 'I feel these People need to be taught a lesson. Changing environments is one thing and sometimes they might think it is for the better, but this poison they spew out is – unforgivable! I say again summon the Cranfield Reds and make sure they come armed.'

The Doss storm

Shane looked at the men. They reminded him of something out of a science fiction film. 'They shouldn't be allowed to burn that stuff, surely that's pollution?'

Dolores could not reply, her whole being felt as if it was hurting inside. So many of the Faeries had been hurt and destroyed and now the men looked determined to annihilate anything that would come near their project.

Dolores' mum agreed with Shane and said she was going to ring the council and tell them what was happening.

Megan was crying.

Nathan stood there with an angry look on his face.

Everyone felt helpless.

As the children looked to the south another swarm arrived to join with the hovering one and together they moved out over the lough towards Ballyronan.

The men went to their diggers, the engines were started up and they began to move towards the Doss Tree.

They thought the swarm was going away.

Suddenly one of the men ran to the diggers, waving his arms and pointing.

The children saw it as well.

The swarm had turned and was coming in over the lough about two metres above the water. In no time it was in amongst the men and this time there were lots of cries. Any part of their body that was exposed was subject to many stinging sensations. Their necks, hands and wrists in particular took painful hits. Eventually one of the men managed to start up one of the leaf blowers and he began to direct the smoke at the part of the swarm which was causing the stings. In their hundreds they began to drop. Then the other blower was started and more and more of the swarm started to break apart and disappear. For what might have been just a few minutes of frantic turmoil finished with what was left of the swarm lifting away from the site. Some of it dispersed to the north and the remainder flowed south.

It was all over.

The men stood there. They took their helmets off. All of them had red spots on their wrists and on their hands if they were not wearing gloves. Their necks were covered and some of them had red spots on their faces. The manager on inspecting everyone said they better get checked out in case of infection, but everyone was to be back early the next morning to begin the work.

'I don't think there will be any more swarms come and bother us.'

The barrels were put out. The diggers were locked up. The men left.

Dolores' Mum had been unable to contact anyone in the Council.

Dolores had not said anything. She turned to go home and when she got there went upstairs and sat looking out her window at the Doss Tree. She had not eaten anything all day. When her Mum went to her room to see if she wanted some supper Dolores had her eyes closed and was rocking herself backwards and forwards. Her Mum gently touched her shoulder.

She opened her eyes, 'I'm OK Mum. The Doss Tree will sort it all out.'

When Shane told his Mum and Dad later about what had happened they had been very supportive and also very angry with Corporate Europe. They condemned the use of the barrels and his Dad said he would call the local politicians tomorrow and make a formal complaint. They both however felt, there was nothing now to be done to stop the development.

Shane, Nathan and Megan went to bed that night very quiet without saying their usual 'goodnight' to their parents. They didn't even have any supper.

The Queen had told the Tree that she was not sure now if there was anything else that could be done. She felt such a failure for not being able to find something that would have made the People change their minds and therefore save the Faerie Hosts. She could not see anything, even when flying with Miach.

The loss of her Faerie Folk was now weighing heavily on her mind.

Eventually the Queen met the Generals at the Skady Tower.

No one said anything.

The Queen was on her black throne, her shoulders slumped forward and her head turned away from her leaders. She could not face them.

It was Fiachra who broke the silence. His voice soft, unusually so for one with so much fire.

'My Queen.'

He rose to his feet.

Black marks covered parts of his person where the oily smoke had clung to him, his wings were badly damaged.

The same was true of all the leaders.

'My Queen. Let us lift our heads high with pride. We all fought valiantly. We lost many good Faerie Folk, they are with our great Earth', he paused, 'there are none among us who should feel ashamed. The shame is on the People and what they did today. Our gifts for battle are such that we can only do so much, we are not the destructive ones. Our hope has always been that when the People decide to change places they will take notice of the things that are dear to us. For too long, as had been said before, they have taken no notice of us. We have always had to compromise, come to terms with their decisions. We have always been pushed aside. Does Dolores understand what has happened today?'

The Queen raised her head and nodded.

'Then leave it in the hands of this child and see if some of the ancient ways can play a role and bring this episode to the right conclusion for the Doss Tree and the lough shore kingdoms.'

By midnight the Doss Tree felt that the People would be safely in their beds. It knew that the special friends it now had were sound asleep. It had brooded long and hard on the events of the day. The destruction of the Faerie Hosts in particular had hurt the tree to its core. It was angry, really, really angry. It was Dolores who had calmed it down, made it realise that the hidden strengths, lying dormant for hundreds of years within its branches and roots, had to come into play and bring about a solution.

Dolores did not need to touch the Doss Tree now to engage with it. The trauma of the days' events had somehow heightened her inner awareness. All she had to do was close her eyes and her senses were able to lock in to the distress of the Doss Tree. As Dolores rocked herself backwards and forwards in her bedroom she felt the anger of the great tree.

'I have had them destroyed. Those gentle, kind, brave Faerie Folk. Yes, even the Doss Devils have loved me. They, who have played among my branches and leaves for the last four hundred years. I had no right to ask. The People are too strong. My time is probably up anyway and I should look forward to that. None of us can go on forever.'

Dolores listened and when the great tree had finished with his anger spoke through her mind.

'Great tree do not distress yourself. The Faerie Hosts have done all they can and it was their choice. No one could have done more. No one could have foreseen the outcome of their engagement.'

'I want to go now. There is nothing left to do. Let the People come tomorrow and destroy me with everything else.'

'This is not the end. Your roots are spread too far and too deep into the ground along the lough shore. I feel there is still something which has not been uncovered and that is for you to find.'

'How can I find something when I do not know what I am looking for?'

'Use your root system, use your branches. We humans do care about many things. The Queen was convinced there was something that could stop this project. She was unable to find it, but, and I believe her, that something is there. Perhaps like many things along the shoreline, hidden away.'

The Doss Tree could sense this change of maturity in Dolores. It began to calm down. Its middle branch stirred and gradually the whole tree began to shake. Its' roots underneath the ground began to vibrate for the first time in its four hundred year life. These roots had spread a great distance from its' central trunk to touch not just the shore edge but ran along the field towards the jetty. Many of the roots were so deep that they ran under the slip road to the jetty and under the house where Dolores lived. There were hundreds of roots running in all directions touching the roots of all the other plants and trees and grasses. Connections were being established that the Doss Tree had forgotten how to touch. A huge underground network of thick roots and thin roots all intertwined. The Doss Tree was asking, asking, touching, seeking, stretching out, through all the land.

What came back to it was an overwhelming, abundance of information. By the time midnight arrived the Doss Tree had processed it all like some gigantic computer and it knew what it had to do.

The Doss storm should help.

A revelation

Everyone in Doss had been wakened by the storm. The weather forecast had not predicted any kind of storm and certainly not one of this ferocity.

Doss was the only place the storm struck.

Later it would be explained away by the experts saying it must have been something to do with the micro climate of the lough. It is well known that localised cyclones can develop if the weather conditions are favourable and could happen anywhere.

Dolores had gone into her parents' room. Together they stood at the window watching the fury of the storm with the moonlight streaming all around it. For all its intensity the storm seemed to concentrate in one particular area. An abandoned fishing boat which had lain broken for a long time on the field suddenly began to move. The Doss Tree was bending and tossing like fury. Dolores could not believe her eyes when the boat appeared to lift off the ground and was tossed onto an overgrown part at the edge of the lough, where it rolled over and over before coming to a stop on the edge of the lough. Suddenly there was an almighty crack and the centre branch of the Doss Tree broke off and fell at the base

George Henry

of the great tree. The storm passed and everything around the shore was bathed in the calm of a moonlit night.

'In all my years of living here,' said Dolores' Dad, 'I have never seen anything like that, not anything.'

'Incredible,' said her Mum shaking her head in disbelief.

'I think when we get up in the morning there may be a revelation,' said Dolores and with that she went back to bed and slept soundly until she was wakened by her Mum.

'Dolores the men are back, and, it looks as if they are going to start working.'

Dolores leapt out of bed and dressed as quickly as she could. When she ran outside, Shane, Nathan and Megan were running down the road towards her house. She shouted to them to hurry up as she ran to the jetty. When her three friends caught up with her they all stood looking at the damaged boat lying on its side in the lough. None of them were looking at the flattened part to the side of it where the overgrown brambles and giant weeds had been.

It was only when Megan said, 'Look at those pretty flowers!', that the others looked and there for all to see were the most beautiful wild orchids.

Dolores turned and raced up to her house.

When she returned with her mum they stood there panting for breath and when she calmed a little asked, 'Well Mum, what do you think?'

With a smile beginning to spread across her face, 'I think my darling girl you may be right. I better speak with the man in charge here before he makes a huge mistake.' And off she ran to the foreman in charge.

As the four children stood watching her have a very animated conversation with the man, Shane blurted out, 'For goodness sake Dolores, what's going on?'

'I think that what's been uncovered by the storm are some very rare orchids, which, if I'm not mistaken, are a protected species on the shores of the Lough Neagh. Lots of other sites have already disappeared and this might turn out to be a new site.'

64

'Is that what the Queen meant?' asked Nathan.

'Yes. She knew there was something but because she has been away for so long and everything on this part of the shore was so overgrown she couldn't quite remember exactly where the orchids were. Another two hundred metres in either direction along the shore, and this wouldn't have mattered. But here comes Mum.'

'Well that gentleman is now on the phone telling his boss what I have just told him. At least he had the sense to tell his men to stop work. I told him that the species is protected under the *1985 Wildlife Order* and he would be breaking the law if they now started clearing the site. What I hope we have here children is what is called 'a priority species'. I told him, don't take my word for it, get an expert. I think as well, for a little bit of insurance, I might just ring the local newspaper', and she smiled mischievously.

They all stood there waiting until the man came and spoke to Dolores' Mum and informed her that they were trying to get someone from the University of Ulster's Biological and Environmental Department to come down and formally identify the orchids. With nothing else to do, a long awaited breakfast was tackled by the children, with much conversation about the night's happenings and the finding of the flowers. Everyone was excited but Dolores added a sombre note, 'I'm worried about the Doss Tree. It was badly damaged in the storm and until those men leave we can't get into the field to see how badly hurt it is.'

It was around lunchtime when a whole fleet of cars arrived in Doss. Men with suits were all over the place. Photographs were being taken and there were many very serious conversations taking place. A reporter had arrived from the *Antrim Guardian* with a camera and a recording device and began interviewing the men in suits.

The workmen on the site looked very amused by everything that was going on.

Eventually a red Volkswagen Beetle car arrived and a bespectacled long haired young man, perhaps in his late twenties, got out. He also had a camera and was directed to where the orchids were. Everyone stood watching him. He took his time to make a very close examination of the orchids. Then, kneeling on one knee, lots of pictures were taken from different angles. When he finished he returned to the assembled group of men with suits and after some discourse returned to his car and left.

The reporter having listened to the young man then approached Dolores' Mum.

'Hi there, I believe you are the lady who rang our paper?'

'Yes, that's correct.'

'It seems you were right. The orchids are a protected species. The guy from the university identified them as,' he rewound his recorder and put it to his ear,' *Spiranthes romanzoffiana*.'

'Down here we call them, *'lady's tresses'.*'

'Did you find them?'

'No it was Megan here, a friend of my daughter. She spotted them first and my Dolores recognised they might be important.'

He recorded more information and then asked if he could take a photograph for the paper.

'This is turning out to be quite a story

When the story appeared it was on the front page with the headline, 'LOUGH NEAGH REVELATION'. The story was not just about the finding of rare orchids it was bigger than that. Other media interests also followed up with television and radio covering the story. Plenty of politicians, from all sides, jumped on the environmental bandwagon until eventually Corporate Europe had been informed by the government that they would have to find an alternative site for their plans.

No more development was to be allowed in Doss.

Like magic

It was some days later before the media began to drift away from the 'orchid story'. Lorries finally arrived to take the diggers and the other equipment away. Dolores and her three friends had not been able to get in to the field to the Doss Tree. Dolores was worried she had not been able to connect with the great tree. Her mum reassured her that things would calm down and when all the fuss was over she and her friends would be back playing around the tree.

Even though she was concerned Dolores had been able to sleep very well since the night of the storm. Many sightseers turned up, especially in the evening, to look at the site of the orchids and to photograph the Doss Tree. The children had stayed away from the field. They were fed up being asked questions. All the people wanted to hear was the story about how the flowers had been uncovered. Dolores and her friends knew the truth of it but didn't want to say, so they kept out of the way. It was three days after the machinery had left that Dolores in a deep sleep was visited by the Queen. When she wakened in the morning she told her Mum and afterwards went to visit her three friends.

'We need to go to the Doss Tree. It is badly hurt and after the energy it expended making the storm it is finding it difficult to get its life force back.'

'Is that why you haven't been able to contact it,' asked Shane.

Dolores nodded her head, 'probably.'

'But what can we do?' asked Nathan.

'We do what Megan said we should do from the beginning – give it a hug.'

'Did the Queen say that if we do that then the Doss Tree will be itself again?'

'The Queen wasn't sure Megan. It felt so bad about causing the destruction of many within the Faerie Hosts that it just might not want to recover. It may feel its time is finished. It has done all it can to protect this part of the lough.'

'Then what are we waiting for,' said Shane, 'let's go.'

The four children hurried down the road, climbed over the gate into the field and approached the Doss Tree. The large centre branch was lying against the base of the tree like some great broken limb. Megan climbed on top of it.

'I'm the smallest and the lightest, so I get to stand on it, that way I'll hurt it the least.'

The others smiled.

Dolores got between Shane and Nathan and held their hands. The two brothers held the hands of their wee sister.

Dolores closed her eyes.

Nothing.

They stood like that for what seemed a long time.

Dolores' Mum came round the front of the house to watch. Then like magic, word spread to the rest of the houses that the Doss Tree needed help. The children from the other homes came out, walked down the road, climbed the gate and approached the Doss Tree. They formed a circle around the tree and stood watching silently as the four friends hugged the ancient tree. Then, as if someone was guiding them to do it, the children moved forward and they all touched one of the four friends hugging the tree. Suddenly, one of the branches began to stir and the leaves gave the faintest rustling sound.

Dolores opened her eyes.

'It's OK, it's going to be all right. The Doss Tree will be with us for a long time to come.'

Later Dolores would tell us that the tree needed an extra source of energy to help it realise that it was greatly loved. The other children all said they had heard a voice and that was why they did what they did. Dolores knew where the voice came from.

Whatever the truth of it, the Doss tree is still there on the shores of Lough Neagh. The large branch that was broken in the storm still lies at the base of the tree. The small jetty for landing the eels remains the same.

And the large eel factory?

Corporate Europe didn't get their hands on it after all.

It actually belongs to the Lough Neagh Fishermens Co-operative Society Ltd. Toomebridge.

If you drive through Toomebridge from the south, then over the old bridge, you can see the factory when you look to your right. It sits on the north side of the River Bann which exits there from Lough Neagh on its' way to the sea. If you are really lucky you might see as many as a dozen Grey Herons, hoping to catch some of those eels.

As for the Faerie thorn tree, it's real alright. You can visit Cranfield Graveyard at Churchtown Point on the shores of Lough Neagh. You'll find the tree near to the old church, still growing, in one of the most tranquil and beautiful parts of this world. And if you happen to be there when the May Fly is about, don't be annoyed by them, for disguised within their swarms might just be some other creatures that we can't quite see.